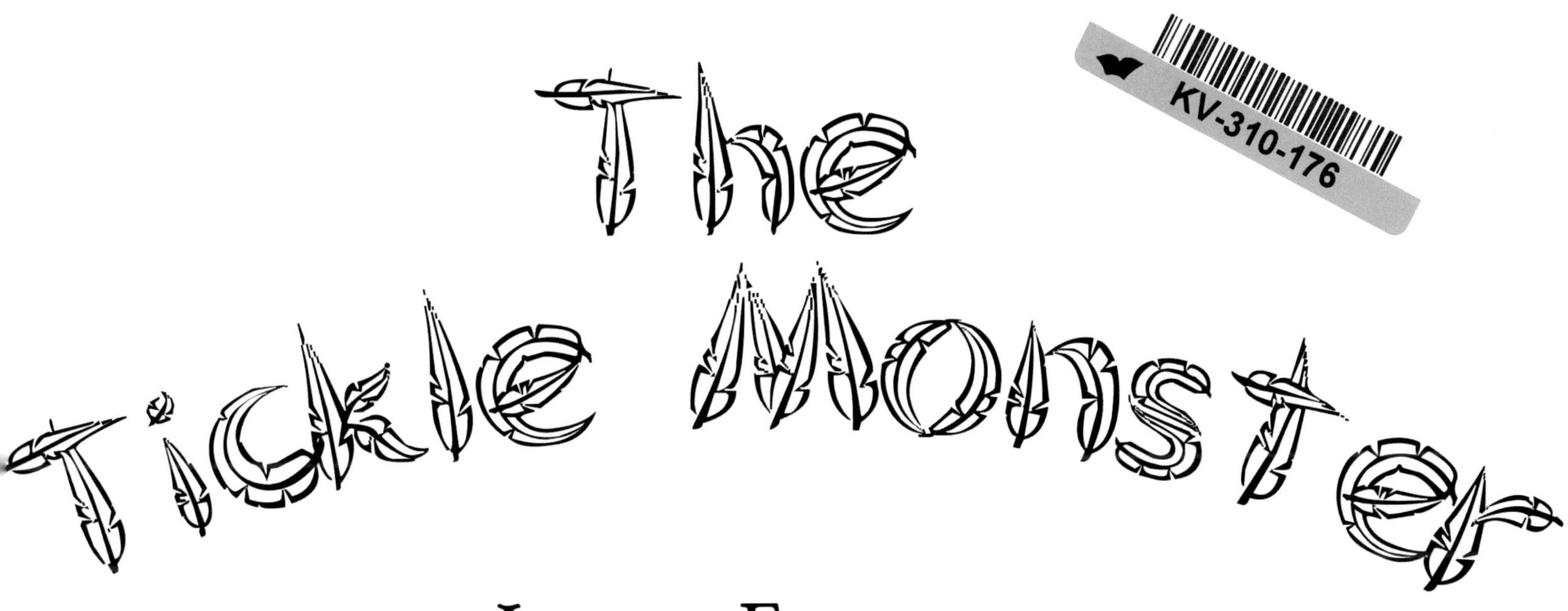




Lorene Farrugia

Benjamin Branding

Underneath the mighty oaks

In a woodland near to me,

Is a wiggly, leafy, narrow path

That darts from tree to tree.

It takes you deep into the woods

Until you find a door,

Where written in squiggly letters

to open,

You must ROaR!

If your roar is loud enough

And if it's any good,

The door will open to welcome you

Into the Monster Wood.

Monster
Wood

The Tickle Monster roams,

Around the Monster Wood.

He looks for things to tickle,

For tickling is good!

With his fingers at the ready,

He's always on the chase.

Tickling everything he can...

# ... he even goes to SPACE!

When on a tickle hunt,

The Tickle Monster's sneaky.

He treads with silent footsteps.

He really is so cheeky!

He searches behind trees,

He rummages under rocks.

Until he spies a monster...

...it's the one who eats your socks!

The Tickle Monster creeps,

As silent as can be.

Upon the busy Sock Monster

Sitting in a tree.

His tickle hands extend

To reach the sock fiend's belly.

And he tickles it with gusto,

Until it wobbles like a jelly!

As giggles fill the woodland air,

The Tickle Monster smiles.

The Sock Monster's loud chuckles

Can be heard for miles and miles!

But one monster is not enough;

He has to tickle more.

So ticklers at the ready,

He sets off to explore.

Deeper in the Monster Wood,

The Tickle Monster sees...

The wheezy, Sneezy Monster,

Looking ill at ease.

The Sneezy Monster sniffs;

His nostrils start to flare.

The Tickle Monster frowns a bit,

He feels he should beware.

He knows it's now or never,

He really musn't linger.

So he takes a few steps closer

And prepares his tickling finger.

Suddenly he sees through trees,

The monster they call BOO!

And grins from ear to ear -

For he can tickle two!

The Tickle Monster thinks

That he is the tickling master.

But this particular tickle

Will end up in disaster.

What he doesn't know is,

That monster they call BOO!

Likes to roar at monsters

To scare them through...

and through!

The Tickle Monster leans, his ticklers at the ready.

The Sneezy Monster shuffles, he looks a bit unsteady.

The tickly feeling starts at the Sneezy Monster's toes...

...and then it's on his legs...

his belly...

...then his nose!

The Tickle Monster laughs whilst the Sneezy Monster wriggles.

Making funny noises, as he giggles and he jiggles.

But naughty monster BOO! arrives with a shake!

She roars the loudest BOO! That makes the woodland

QUAKE!

The poor old Sneezy Monster, he knows not what to do.

Then suddenly, no warning

He gives a loud...

ATCHO

It is the biggest sneeze the monsters have ever heard.

It blows away the leaves and all the Rainbow birds.

Those very silly monsters – they should have had more care!

A fact that they once realised,

Whilst soaring through the air!

As for Sneezy Monster, that Tickle and that BOO!

Had made him sneeze and sneeze and sneeze...

The Tickle Monster tries

To be more careful now.

And doesn't get too greedy

When on a tickling prowl.

He never saw again the

Monster they call BOO!

And steers well clear of

Sneezy Monster –

avoiding that ...

**ATCHOO!**

The End